The Thirsty Saguaro

by Amber Garcia

Illustrated by the author

The Thirsty Saguaro

Copyright © 2020 by Amber Garcia

ISBN: 978-0-9817939-8-6 (hard cover)

ISBN: 978-0-9817939-7-9 (soft cover)

1st Edition Nov. 2020
Printed in the USA by
Three Knolls Publishing & Printing, Tucson, AZ
www.3knollspub.com

There once was a thirsty saguaro that just couldn't get enough to drink.

While all the other
saguaros craved
sunshine, he wished
only for rain.
The desert didn't
seem to be the right
place for this
thirsty saguaro.

He constantly dreamed of living in a rainforest or maybe rooted by a beautiful lake.

But every
day he would
wake to
find he was
still standing
in the dry,
dusty desert
with the sun
shining
bright.

Then one day,
he felt a drop of
something cool
and wet fall on
his head.
At first, he
thought it was
just another
bird. But then
he felt
another drop
and another.

He looked up
and just like
that, RAIN.
The drops were
big and wet
and delicious!
It was glorious!

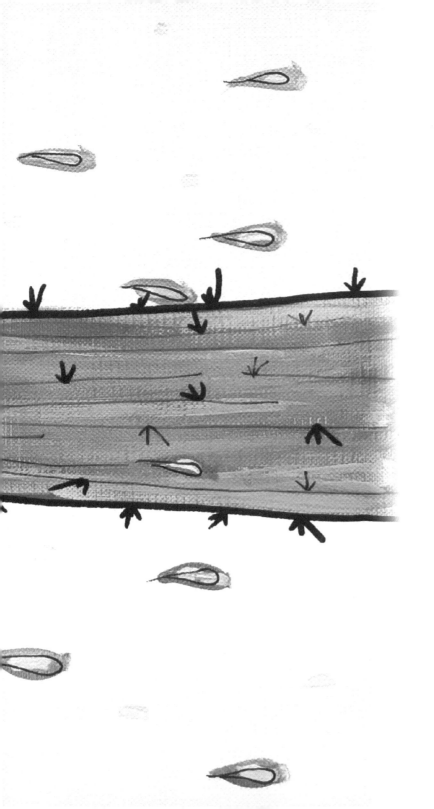

He tilted his head back and he reached up high and stretched his arms out as far as he could, catching all those cool rain drops with every prick and thorn he had, trying to drink it all up.

By the time the rain
stopped he was
no longer thirsty!
He was happy,
and he could
hardly wait for it to
rain again.

Good Night Sun

Another day of shining over the
desert has come to an end
It's time for you to settle in behind
the mountains under the
blanket of stars
As you pull up the covers and
tuck yourself in,
the sky changes colors and
the stars start to glisten
Good night sun, the moon will glow
through the night until you rise
and shine bright again

We hope you enjoyed The Thirsty Saguaro.

Look for more Saguaro Tales:

Saguaros Can't Wear Pants

Sheriff Saguaro

CPSIA information can be obtained
at www.ICGtesting.com
Printed in the USA
LVHW071947291020
670161LV00012B/451